CICADA

SHAUN TAN

ARTHUR A. LEVINE BOOKS
An Imprint of Scholastic Inc.

Cicada work in tall building.

Data entry clerk. Seventeen year.

No sick day. No mistake.

Tok Tok Tok!

Seventeen year. No promotion.

Human resources say cicada not human.

Need no resources.

Tok Tok Tok!

No cicada allowed in office bathroom.

Cicada go downtown. Twelve blocks.

Each time company dock pay.

Tok Tok Tok!

Human never finish work.

Cicada always stay late. Finish work.

Nobody thank cicada.

Tok Tok Tok!

Human coworker no like cicada.

Say things. Do things.

Think cicada stupid.

Tok Tok Tok!

Cicada no afford rent.

Live in office wall space.

Company pretend not know.

Tok Tok Tok!

Seventeen year. Cicada retire.

No party. No handshake.

Boss say clean desk.

Tok Tok Tok!

No work. No home. No money.

Cicada go to top of tall building.

Time to say goodbye.

Tok Tok Tok!

Cicada all fly back to forest.

Sometimes think about human.

Can't stop laughing.

Tok Tok Tok!

閑かさや
岩にしみ入る
蝉の声

calm and serene

the sound of a cicada

penetrates the rock

Matsuo Bashō (1644–94)
translation by Yuzuru Miura

Library of Congress Cataloging-in-Publication Data available

ISBN 978-1-338-29839-0

10 9 8 7 6 5 4 3 2 1   19 20 21 22 23

Printed in China   62
This edition first printing, February 2019

Book design by Shaun Tan and Phil Falco
Art photography by Matthew Stanton

The text type was set in Helvetica Neue.
The display type was set in Heiti.
The illustrations were created using oil on canvas and paper.